И. Б.
1907.

RUSSIAN FAIRY TALES

Литература

Literatura Publishers
MOSCOW
2000

ББК 84(2)
Р89

Russian fairy tales

Complited by A. Afanasiev
Illustrations by I. Bilibin
Translated from Russian by A. Zamchuk

CONTENTS

This book has been exclusively for:

BABUSHKA, Inc.

333 Jefferson Street, #126
San Francisco, CA 94133 USA
Tel. (415) 673 6740
Fax (650) 941 8107

ISBN 5-7842-0107-7

Sister Alionushka and brother Ivanushka

Once upon a time there lived a tsar and tsaritsa and they had a son and a daughter named Ivanushka and Alionushka. After the tsar's and tsaritsa's death they remained alone and went wrambling all over the world.

They walked and walked until they saw a pond with a herd of cows grazing around.

«I am thirsty,» said Ivanushka.

«Don't drink it, brother, otherwise you will turn to a calf,» said Alionushka.

He listened to her and they went on further. They walked and walked and came up to a river and saw herd of horses near it.

«Ah, sister, I am so thirsty. If you could only know it.»

«Don't drink it, brother, otherwise you will turn to a colt.»

Ivanushka listened to her, and they went on further. They walked and walked and saw a lake with a herd of sheep near it.

«Ah, sister, I shall drink. So thirsty I am.»

«Don't drink, brother, otherwise you will turn to a lamb.»

Ivanushka listened to her and they went on further. They walked and walked and saw some pigs near the pond.

«Ah, sister, I shall drink. I am so much thirsty.»

«Don't drink, brother, otherwise you will turn to a piglet.»

Ivanushka listened to her again, they went straight ahead walked and saw a herd of goats grazing near water.

«Ah, sister, this time I must drink.»

«Don't drink, brother, or you will turn to a kid.»

But that time he couldn't restrain himself from drinking and didn't listen to the sister. He drank some water and turned to a kid. He started jumping before Alionushka and crying:

«Mee-ke-ke! mee-ke-ke!»

Alionushka tied him up with a silken belt and led him after her, crying and crying bitterly.

The kid was running and running till he ran to some tsar's garden. As soon as people saw him they, at once, reported to the tsar.

«Your Majesty. There is a kid in your garden and a maiden who is so nice leads him on a belt.»

The tsar ordered them to find out where she hailed from. The servants asked Alionushka where from she was and who her parents were.

«My parents were a tsar and tsaritsa, but they are dead,» said Alionushka. «And we are their children — me, the tsarevna, and this is my brother, the tsarevich. He couldn't restrain himself from drinking some water and turned to a kid.»

The people told the tsar all that. The tsar invited Alionushka and questioned her about everything himself. The tsar decided to marry her because be liked her very much. At once they got married and started living together and the kid lived with them. The kid walked in the garden and ate and drank together with the tsar and tsaritsa.

Once the tsar left for hunting meanwile a sorceress came to the palace and cast a spell upon the tsaritsa. Alionushka fell ill and turned very thin and pale. Everything got gloomy in the palace. All the flowers, trees and grass started fading, drying up and withering.

«Aren't you well?» the tsar asked Alionushka when returned to the palace from hunting.

«Yes, I have fallen ill,» answered the tsaritsa.

Next day when the tsar left for hunting again the sorceress came up to the palace and found Alionushka being ill.

«Do you want me to cure you? Go to a certain sea at twilight and drink water there.»

The tsaritsa obeyed her and came up to the sea. The sorceress who was waiting for her there, grabbed her, tied up a stone to her neck and threw her into the sea. The kid ran up to the sea and cried very bitterly. The sorceress turned into Alionushka and went back to the palace.

The tsar was overfilled with joy having found the tsaritsa well again. They set the table and sat down for dinner.

«But I don't see our kid. Where is he?» asked the tsar.

«I gave orders to never let him in. He reeks with goat so much!»

Next day, as soon as the tsar left for hunting again, the sorceress seized the kid and started beating him with the following words:

«As soon as the tsar returns back from hunting I'll tell him to stab you.»

When the tsar got back to the palace she pestered him, «Order to stab the kid. I am so disgusted by him that I can't see him any more!»

The tsar liked the kid so much but there was nothing to do. She kept on insisting on the kid to be stabbed that finally the tsar gave such a permission.

The kid saw that steel knives were being sharpened and wept.

He ran up to the tsar and asked, «Tsar! Let me go the sea — shore and rinse my guts.»

The tsar let him go. The kid went to the sea shore and implored:

Alionushka, sister of mine,
Get up, get up to the shore!

> Hot fires are being burnt,
> Huge pots are being boiled.
> They are sharpening the steel knives
> They are willing to stab me!

Alionushka answered him:

> Ivanushka, brother of mine!
> A heavy stone drags me down to the bottom,
> A sepulchural snake sucked my heart out!

And the kid got back to the palace. At the midday he came to the tsar and started begging him to let him go to the sea and rinse his guts again.

The tsar let him go. The kid returned to the sea and started calling Alionushka again:

> Alionushka, sister of mine,
> Get up, get up to the shore!
> Hot fires are being burnt,
> Huge pots are being boiled.
> They are sharpening the steel knives
> They are willing to stab me!

Alionushka answered him:

> Ivanushka, brother of mine!
> A heavy stone drags me down to the bottom,
> A sepulchural snake sucked my heart out!

The kid returned home with the same result. The tsar thought: «What could this mean? Why the kid keeps on running to the sea shore?»

So the kid implored for the third time, «Tsar! Let me go to the sea and rinse my guts one more time!»

The tsar allowed him to go and decided to follow the kid himself. He came up to the sea and heard the kid crying:

> Alionushka, sister of mine,
> Get up, get up to the shore!
> Hot fires are being burnt,
> Huge pots are being boiled.
> They are sharpening the steel knives
> They are willing to stab me!

Alionushka answered him:

> Ivanushka, brother of mine!
> A heavy stone drags me down to the bottom,
> A sepulchural snake sucked my heart out!

The kid kept on calling her until she finally swam up to the surface of the sea. The tsar grabbed Alionushka, tore the stone off her neck and asked how everything had happened. She told him everything. The tsar was filled up with joy the same as the kid was. When three of them returned to the palace the garden started blossoming again.

As to the sorceress she was ordered to be punished. The flame was in the courtyard because the sorceress was burnt on it. The tsar with his wife and the kid started living happily, and eating and drinking together as before.

Сказка
об
Иване-царевиче,
Жар-птице и
о сером волке.

Tale of Ivan-Tsarevich, the firebird and the grey wolf

Once upon a time in a certain tsardom, in a certain state there lived a tsar named Vyslav Andronovich. He had three sons. The first was Tsarevich Dmitry, the second Tsarevich Vasily and the third Tsarevich Ivan.

Tsar Vyslav Andronovich had a garden and the garden was so rich that there was no one better in any other tsardom.

All types of precious trees with and without fruit grew in this garden. One apple tree was the tsar's beloved. All the apples of the tree were of pure gold.

A firebird fell into the habit to fly to Vyslav's garden. It's wings were of gold and eyes resembled oriental crystals. Every night it flew over the garden, perched on Tsar Vyslav's favourite apple tree and picked some golden apples and took off.

Tsar Vyslav Andronovich was very much upset about so many apples had been stolen by the firebird.

Once he challenged three sons of his and said, «My beloved sons! The one of you who will manage to catch the firebird will inherit a half of my tsardom during my lifetime and all the rest after my death.»

Then his sons-tsareviches explained in one voice, «Your Majesty! Our beloved Dad! With great diligence we will do our best to catch the firebird alive.»

The first night Tsarevich Dmitry went to keep watch over the garden. He sat under the apple tree from which the firebird was stealing apples, fell asleep and didn't hear the firebird come and pick very many apples.

9

In the morning Vyslav Andronovich called his son Tsarevich Dmitry and asked, «Well, my dear son. Did you see the firebird or not?»

He answered, «No, my beloved Dad! It didn't come last night.»

The next night Tsarevich Vasily went to the garden. He sat under the apple tree, fell asleep and didn't hear how the firebird came and picked some apples.

In the morning Tsar Vyslav called his son and asked, «Well, my dear son. Did you see the firebird or not?»

«No, my beloved Dad. It didn't come last night.»

The third night Tsarevich Ivan went to the garden and sat under the apple tree. By the time he had been waiting for three hours, a sudden light illuminated the garden as if it were many fires. The firebird came, sat on the tree and started picking the apples.

Tsarevich Ivan sneaked up to the firebird so softly that managed to seize it's tail. But he was unable to hold it. The firebird broke out from him and flew away, but left feather of it's tail he held very fast in his hand.

Next morning, as soon as Tsar Vyslav was awaken by the daylight, Tsarevich Ivan gave him the firebird's feather.

Tsar Vyslav was very happy that his youngest son managed to get at least one firebird's feather.

This feather was so nice and bright that if it had been taken to a dungeon, it would have been so light down there as if many candles had been fired. Tsar Vyslav put the feather in his chamber and treated it as if it were a sort of thing to be kept forever. Since then the firebird never came to the garden.

Tsar Vyslav again challenged his sons and said to them, «My dear sons! Go blessed by me, find the firebird and bring it back to me alive. And what I have promised before the one of you will get who manages to bring the firebird to me.»

Tsarevich Dmitry and Tsarevich Vasily started bearing malice toward their younger brother, that he had managed to tear off the feather from the firebird's tail. They accepted their Dad's blessing and took off together to look for the firebird.

Tsarevich Ivan also began to ask for his Dad's blessing.

Tsar Vyslav told him, «My dear son, my sweet child! You are too young and unskilled for such a long and difficult journey. Why would you leave me? Your brothers have gone already. What would be with me if three of you left and weren't back for a long time? I am old enough and walk beneath God. Who will rule the tsardom if God takes my life? Then there might be a riot and discord among our people there would be nobody to pacify them. There also would be nobody to govern our armies if an enemy invaded our land.»

Though notwithstanding that tsar Vyslav tried very hard to keep his youngest son home, so persistent his begging was that the tsar had to let him go. Tsarevich Ivan accepted his Dad's blessing, chose a horse and hit the road. And he rode being unaware of where he went.

He was breaking his way. But whether it was close or far or low or high, the story is been soon told but never a deed being done soon.

At last he arrived at wide fields, green meadows. And stumbled upon a pillar with the following words on it:

«The one who goes ahead from this pillar will be hungry and cold. The one who goes to the right will be healthy and strong but his horse will be dead. And the one who goes to the left will die himself but his horse will stay alive.»

Tsarevich Ivan read this inscription and turned to the right, having in mind that although his horse would be slayed, he himself would stay alive and, in some time, he might manage to get another horse.

He was riding one day, another and on the third day, all of a sudden, a huge grey wolf came out from the forest and said to Ivan, «Oh, fine youth, Ivan Tsarevich! Surely you have read what was written on the pillar. That your horse would be dead. So why have you taken this way?»

After uttering these words the wolf tore Tsarevich Ivan's horse in two parts and was gone.

Tsarevich Ivan grieved for his horse very much, cried bitterly and went ahead on foot. He was walking all day and got very much tired. When he was about to sit down for rest, suddenly the grey wolf caught up with him.

«I feel sorry for you, Ivan Tsarevich. You have so much exhausted yourself. I wish I hadn't eaten your kind horse. All right! Sit on my grey wolf's back and say where you are to be taken and why.»

Tsarevich Ivan told the wolf where he had to be taken. The grey wolf raced along with him faster than any horse and, in a while, by night, he brought Tsarevich Ivan to a stone wall not very high.

He stopped and said, «Well, Tsarevich Ivan. Get of my grey wolf's back and climb over this wall. There is a tsar's garden beyond the wall in which the firebird sits in a golden cage. If you take a gold cage you will never leave the garden. You will be caught by guards immediately.»

Tsarevich Ivan climbed over the wall and got right into the garden, saw the firebird inside the cage and became very attracted by it. He took the firebird out of the cage and went back with it.

Then he fell to thinking and said to himself, «Why have I taken the firebird without the cage? Where will I put it?»

As soon as be took the cage and was about leaving all of a sudden a great thunder and clatter began throughout the garden. Strings had been tied up to the cage.

The guards were woken up at once, caught Tsarevich Ivan up and brought him to their tsar named Dolmat.

Tsar Dolmat got into a fury and yelled at Tsarevich Ivan in a loud and very angry voice, «Shame of you, young thief! Who are you, from what land, whose father's son and what is your name?»

Tsarevich Ivan told him, «I am from Vyslav's tsardom, Tsar Vyslav's son. And my name is Tsarevich Ivan. Your firebird fell into habit to fly to our garden each night. It picked golden apples from my Dad's favourite tree and spoiled almost the whole tree. For that reason Vyslav Andronovich sent me to find the firebird and bring it to him.»

«Oh, young Tsarevich Ivan,» said Tsar Dolmat. «Is it correct to do what you have done? If you had come to me, you would have received the firebird with my respects. And now would it be good if I sent my word to all the tsars on how dishonestly you have acted in my tsardom. However, listen, Tsarevich Ivan! If you do me a service, if you go beyond thirty lands, to the thirtieth tsardom and get to me the golden-maned steed belonging to Tsar Afron, I will forgive you and the firebird will be my present to you. But if you fail to do this service, I shall send my word to any tsardom that you are a dishonerable thief.»

Tsarevich Ivan left the Tsar Dolmat land in great sadness, having promised to get the steed with a golden mane.

He went to the grey wolf and told him everything that Tsar Dolmat had said to him.

«Oh, young Tsarevich Ivan! Why didn't you listen to me and took the golden cage?» said the grey wolf.

«I am guilty before you,» said Tsarevich Ivan.

«All right, let it be like this,» said the grey wolf. «Climb on my back and I'll take you where you have to be.»

Tsarevich Ivan climbed on grey wolf's back and the wolf was racing as fast as an arrow. And he ran, whether long or not, finally at night he came to Tsar Afron's tsardom.

Having reached the white-stoned royal stables, the grey wolf said to Tsarevich Ivan, «Go, Tsarevich Ivan, into these white-stoned stables. Now all the grooms are sleeping. But there is a golden bridle hanging on the wall. Don't touch it, otherwise it will be the worse for you!»

Tsarevich Ivan entered a white-stoned stables, took the steed and was about coming back when he noticed the golden bridle hanging on the wall. He was so enchanted by it that he removed the bridle from its nail. Just as he did it, a horrible clatter and thunder began through the stables, because the strings had been tied up to the bridle.

The grooms were woken up at once and they rushed in. They seized Tsarevich Ivan and brought him to Tsar Afron.

Tsar Afron started questioning him.

«Young man! Tell me who you are, from what land, who's father's son and what your name is?»

Tsarevich Ivan answered, «I am from Vyslav's tsardom. I am the son of Tsar Vyslav Andronovich and I am Tsarevich Ivan.»

«Oh, young man, Tsarevich Ivan! Does what you have done befit an honourable knight? If you had come to me I would have given to you the steed with the golden mane with my respects. But now if I sent my word how you have acted at my lands to every tsardom how you would like it? However, listen, Tsarevich Ivan! If you do a deed for me, if you go beyond thirty land to the thirtieth tsardom and fetch for me Princess Elena the Beautiful,

14

whom I have been loving, heart and soul, for so long, but whom I am unable to get, your fault will be forgiven and the steed with the golden mane will be my honourable present to you. But if you fail to do this service, than what you have done and that you are dishonourable thief will be proclaimed in all the lands,» said Tsar Afron.

Then Tsarevich Ivan promised Tsar Afron to get Princess Elena the Beautiful to the tsar, left his chamber and wept bitterly.

He went to the grey wolf and told him everything that had happened to him.

«Oh, young man, Tsarevich Ivan!» said the grey wolf. «Why didn't you listen to my words? What for did you take the golden bridle?»

«I am guilty before you,» said Tsarevich Ivan.

«All right, let it be like this!» said the grey wolf. «Climb on my back and I will take you to where you have to be.»

Tsarevich Ivan climbed on the grey wolf's back and the wolf was racing as fast as an arrow. And he ran, like in a tale to be said, not that long and finally arrived in the tsardom of Princess Elena the Beautiful.

Having reached the golden fence surrounding the remarkable garden, the wolf said to Tsarevich Ivan, «Now, Tsarevich Ivan, get down from me and go back along the same road we were running here. Wait for me in the wide field under the green oak.»

Tsarevich Ivan went where he was ordered. The grey wolf sat close to the golden fence and began waiting for Princess to go for a walk in the garden.

By the evening, when the sun was setting to the West and the air was fresh, Princess Elena the Beautiful went out to for a walk into the garden with nannies and governesses. When she entered the garden and was coming closer to the place where the wolf was waiting behind the fence, the grey wolf suddenly jumped over the fence into the garden and seized Princess Elena the Beautiful. He jumped back over the fence and ran with her on top of his force.

He ran into the wide field to the green oak, where Tsarevich Ivan was waiting for him and said, «Tsarevich Ivan, very quickly climb on my grey wolf's back!»

Tsarevich Ivan climbed on the grey wolf's back and he rushed with two of them toward Tsar Afron's lands.

The nannies and governesses who had accompanied Elena the Beautiful during the walk in the garden ran at once to the palace and sent the guards to overtake the grey wolf. But no matter how fast they were they failed to catch them and they returned back to the palace.

Tsarevich Ivan and Elena the beautiful, sitting on the grey wolf's back, have fallen in love with each other with all their hearts.

When they finally reached the Tsar Afron's tsardom and Tsarevich Ivan had to lead Princess Elena the Beautiful to the palace and pass her to Tsar Afron, he was extremely dissapointed and burnt into bitter tears.

The grey wolf asked him, «Why are you weeping, Tsarevich Ivan?»

Tsarevich Ivan answered, «Grey wolf, friend of mine! How should I not weep and sorrow? I love Elena the Beautiful with all my heart, and now I have to give her to Tsar Afron and get from him the horse with the golden mane, otherwise he will dishonour me throughout all the lands.»

«I have served much for you, Tsarevich Ivan,» said the grey wolf, «and I will serve this one as well for you. Listen to me, Tsarevich Ivan. I will turn myself into the Elena the Beautiful and you lead me to Tsar Afron and get a steed with a golden mane in return. He will take me as a real princess. And when you ride the steed with a golden mane and it will take you far from the Tsar Afron tsardom, I will beg him for letting me out for a walk in the wide field. And when he lets me out with nannies and governesses and all the courtiers, and I am in the wide field, just remember me and I shall be again with you.»

The grey wolf said these words to Tsarevich Ivan, struck himself against the earth, and turned into Princess Elena the Beautiful, so that nobody would ever have a shade of doubt it were not her.

Tsarevich Ivan took the grey wolf, went to Tsar Afron's palace and ordered Elena the Beautiful to wait for him outside the town.

When Tsarevich Ivan came to Tsar Afron with phoney Elena the Beautiful, than tsar was overfilled with happiness to get the treasure for which he had been waiting so long. He accepted the phoney princess in return for the steed with the golden mane.

И. БИЛИБИНЪ. 1899.

Tsarevich Ivan mounted the steed and rode out of town. He let the princess mount on the steed's back and headed for the Tsar Dolmat's tsardom.

The grey wolf lived at Tsar Afron's palace one day, another, the third day, and on the fourth, he went to Tsar Afron and started begging the tsar to let him out for a walk to the wide field, to disperse his wild sadness.

Tsar Afron said to him, «Ah, my beautiful Elena! I will do everything for you and I will let you go out for a walk in the wide field.»

And he right away ordered nannies and the governesses to accompany the beautiful princess in the wide field.

Tsarevich was riding along the road together with Elena the Beautiful and talking to her. He forgot about the grey wolf but later he remembered.

«Ah, where is my grey wolf?»

All of a sudden, as soon as he remembered the grey wolf, he showed up before Tsarevich Ivan and said, «Tsarevich Ivan, climb on my back, and let Elena the Beautiful ride on the steed with the golden mane.»

Tsarevich Ivan mounted on the grey wolf's back and they rode to the Tsar Dolmat's tsardom.

Whether they travelled for a long time or not, they arrived at the tsardom and stopped three versts from the town.

Tsarevich Ivan started imploring the grey wolf, «Listen, grey wolf, friend of mine! You have done big deal of a job for me. Than do the last service for me. And this service will be the following. Aren't you able to turn into a horse with a golden mane instead of this one? I don't want to part with this steed with golden mane.»

All of a sudden the grey wolf struck himself against the damp earth and turned into a steed with a golden mane.

Having left Princess Elena the Beautiful in a green meadow, Tsarevich Ivan mounted the grey wolf's back and set out for to the Tsar Dolmat's palace. And when they came there, Tsar Dolmat saw Tsarevich Ivan riding on the steed with the golden mane, and he was overjoyed and left his chamber right away. He met Tsarevich Ivan in his wide courtyard, kissed him in his sweet lips, took him by the right hand and let him into the white-stoned palace.

Tsar Dolmat ordered to create a great feast to celebrate such a gladness and they sat at oaken tables adorned by the sumptuous table clothes. They were eating, drinking and having fun for two days. On the third day Tsar Dolmat handed the firebird in the golden cage to Tsarevich Ivan.

The tsarevich took the firebird, went outside of town, mounted the horse with the golden mane together with Elena the Beautiful, and left for his fatherland, the tsardom of Tsar Vyslav Andronovich.

The next day it occured to Tsar Dolmat to sample his gold-maned steed in the wide field. Ordered to have the steed saddled, mounted it. But the steed with the golden mane threw him down, turned back into the grey wolf and pushed away to catch up with Tsarevich Ivan.

«Tsarevich Ivan,» said the grey wolf, «climb on my grey wolf's back and let Elena the Beautiful ride the steed with the golden mane.»

Tsarevich Ivan sat on the grey wolf and they took their way. As soon as they reached the place where the grey wolf tore the horse of Ivan Tsarevich, he stopped.

«Well, Tsarevich Ivan,» said the grey wolf. «I have served to you long in faith and truth. Right here I have torn your horse in two and I have taken you right to this spot. Dismount me, the grey wolf. Now you have the gold-maned steed. Ride on it wherever you need. I am not your servant any more.»

The grey wolf said these words and ran aside. Tsarevich Ivan burnt into bitter tears over the grey wolf and together with princess Elena set out for his native land.

Whether for a long time or short he rode together with Princess Elena the Beautiful on steed with the golden mane, finally they stopped still about twenty versts from the native town. They dismounted the steed and lay down together to rest from the intense heat under the tree. He tied the steed with the gold mane to the same tree and put the cage with the firebird in it close to him.

Lying on the soft grass and holding amorous talks to each other they have fallen asleep.

At that time the brothers of Tsarevich Ivan, Tsarevich Dmitry and Tsarevich Vasily, who travelled much in all the tsardoms and didn't find the firebird, were riding back to their native land empty-handed. By chance they stumbled upon their sleeping brother, who was lying beside Princess Elena the Beautiful.

When they saw the steed with the gold mane and the firebird in the golden cage, they were much enticed with a thought of killing their brother.

Tsarevich Dmitry took his sword from the sheath, stabbed Tsarevich Ivan and hacked him to pieces. Then he awoke Princess Elena the Beautiful and started questioning her.

«Sweetest maiden! From what tsardom have you come? Who's father's are you daughter and what is your name?»

Princess Elena the Beautiful was horribly frightened when she saw Tsarevich Ivan lying dead. She wept bitterly.

She said crying, «I am Princess Elena the Beautiful. I was saved by Tsarevich Ivan, whom you have put to the evil death. You would have been valiant knights if you had gone onto the wide field and slayed him honesty. But you have done it when he was asleep, and there is no pride in it. A sleeping man is the same as dead man!»

Then Tsarevich Dmitry set his sword against the heart of beautiful Princess Elena and told her, «Listen to me, Elena the Beautiful! You are in our hands now. We will take you to our Dad, Tsar Vyslav Andronovich, and you shall tell him that we have procured you as well as the firebird and the golden-maned steed. If you don't say this, I shall finish you at once!»

The beautiful princess was frightened by death and started promising and swearing by everything sacred that would be speaking as she was ordered.

Then Tsarevich Dmitry and Tsarevich Vasily cast lots to see who should get the Beautiful Elena and who should get the golden-maned steed. The lots showed the beautiful Elena must go to Tsarevich Vasily and the steed with the golden mane to Tsarevich Dmitry.

Then Tsarevich Vasily took the beautiful princess and put her on his good horse. Tsarevich Dmitry mounted the horse with the golden mane and took cage with the firebird to hand it to his parent, Tsar Vyslav Andronovich. They set out for their palace.

Tsarevich Ivan was laying dead exactly thirty days on the ground by the time when the grey wolf stumbled upon him and recognized him by his scent. The grey wolf wanted to help him out, to revive him, but didn't know how to do it.

Just at that time, the grey wolf noticed a raven and two young ravens flying over the dead body and willing to come down and to eat the flesh of Tsarevich Ivan.

The grey wolf hid himself behind the bushes and as soon as the young ravens swooped down and started pecking the flesh of Tsarevich Ivan, he rushed out of the bushes, seized one of two young ravens and was about to tear it in two. Then the raven sat on the ground at some distance from the grey wolf and said to him, «Oh, grey wolf, don't touch my young child. He's done nothing bad to you.»

«Listen, raven,» said the grey wolf, «I shan't touch your child and it will leave unharmed if you will do a service for me. Fly beyond the thirty land, to the thirtieth tsardom and bring me some dead and life water.»

To that the raven said the following, «I will do this service for you. Just don't harm my child.»

Having pronounced these words the raven took off and soon got out of sight.

On the third day the raven flew back carrying two phials. One contained the life water, another the water for death. He handed these phials to the grey wolf.

The grey wolf took the phials and tore the little raven in two. He sprinkled him with the dead water first, and the raven's parts got together. Then with life water — and the raven recovered.

Then the grey wolf sprinkled the body of Tsarevich Ivan firstly with the dead water and it grew together. Then he sprinkled him with life water and Tsarevich Ivan stood up.

«Oh, so long I have slept!»

The grey wolf answered him, «Tsarevich Ivan, if it had not been for me you would have slept forever. Your brothers hacked you to pieces and took with them Princess Elena the Beautiful, the golden-maned steed and the firebird. Now go as fast as you can to your native tsardom. Your brother, Tsarevich Vasily, is about to marry the Beautiful Elena your bride. To get to there faster you better climb on my grey wolf's back.»

Tsarevich Ivan mounted the grey wolf and he ran to the tsardom of the Tsar Vyslav Andronovich and in either a short time or a long time they reached the town.

Tsarevich Ivan dismounted the grey wolf and went to the town. When he entered the palace there was a great feast there and celebration of the wedding of his brother Tsarevich Vasily and Princess Elena the Beautiful. No sooner had Elena the Beautiful seen Tsarevich Ivan, she rushed to him and began to kiss his sweet lips, and cried out, «This is my beloved bridegroom, but not the villain who sits at the table!»

Then the Tsar Vyslav Andronovich got up from his seat and started questioning Elena the Beautiful as to what could it meant of what she had said. Elena the Beautiful told all the truth about what had happened. How Tsarevich Ivan had got her, the golden-maned steed and the firebird; how his older brothers had slayed him when he was sleeping and scared her to make her say that they had got all that.

Tsar Vyslav Andronovich was terribly crossed with his older sons and ordered to throw them to the dungeon. Tsarevich Ivan married Princess Elena the Beautiful and they lived in true love and friendship and no one of them could spend a single minute without the other's presence.

Vasilisa the Beautiful

There lived a merchant in a certain tsardom. This merchant had lived twelve years with his beloved wife and had only one daughter, who's name was Vasilisa the Beautiful.

When the merchant's wife was dying, she called her daughter, took a doll from under her blanket, gave it to her and said, «Listen to me, Vasilisushka! Remember and fulfil my last words. I am dying and together with my maternal blessing I am leaving to you this doll. Keep it and never show it to anybody. And if some trouble gets you feed the doll and ask for it's advice. After it has eaten, it will advice you how to overcome the misfortune.»

Then the mother kissed her daughter and died.

After the death of his wife the merchant grieved and started thinking of new marriage.

He was a good man. There was no shortage of brides, but he loved some widow best. She was elderly already and had two daughters of her own, who were approximately of the same age with Vasilisa. So she was supposed to be an experienced mother and housewife.

So he got married the widow, but be deceived himself, for she was never good mother for Vasilisa.

Vasilisa was the first beauty in the village. Her stepmother together with sisters envied her beauty, tormented her with all kinds of toil so that she would get thinner and grow black from the wind and sun.

So, her life was really a hardship.

But Vasilisa bore all of that without a murmur and was getting more and more beautiful and plumper from day to day.

23

Meanwhile, the stepmother with her daughters were growing thinner and uglier from malice. Though, they never laboured and always sat with their hands folded, as if they were ladies.

How could it be like this?

Vasilisa was helped by her doll. Without this she would have never been able to manage all that hassles!

Though, it happened that Vasilisa stayed hungry herself, but the doll was always stuffed.

At night, when everyone was asleep, she would lock herself in the small room where she lived and would treat her doll, saying, «Eat, my little doll! Listen to my trouble. I live in my Dad's house but see no joy. My malicious stepmother hounds me to death. Would you tell me how I should live and what I should do.»

The doll would eat first, then would give her advice and calm her down.

And in the morning, she would do all job for Vasilisa.

Vasilisa just rested in the shade and plucked flowers, and by this time all the vegetable patches were weeded, the cabbage sprayed, the water brought in the house, the oven burned.

The doll would ever show Vasilisa the sun protecting herb.

It was an easy living with the doll. Several years passed. Vasilisa grew up and became a bride.

She was wooed by each youngster in the village, and no one even glanced at her stepmother's daughters.

The stepmother was getting more and more angry, and she answered everybody, «I'll not let the youngest daughter marry before the elder ones!»

After next suitor was gone she wreaked her anger on Vasilisa by beating her.

Once there came a day when the merchant had to leave for rather long time on some business.

The stepmother began to live in another house.

A thick forest was near this house, and there was a little hut in a glade of the forest.

In the hut lived Baba Yaga.

She allowed nobody to come close to her and ate people as if they were chickens.

After the stepmother moved to a new house, she always sent the hated Vasilisa to the forest. But each time she returned home safe and sound.

Her doll showed the way to her and never let her approach the hut where Baba Yaga lived.

Autumn came. The stepmother gave all the three maidens their evening works. One was made weave the lace, the other had to knit stockings and Vasilisa had to spin.

She put out all the lights in the house except one candle where the maidens worked, and fell asleep.

The girls worked. One of stepmother's daughters took the scissors to trim the attic and, as if she did it occasionally, but indeed following her mother's order, she extinguished the fire.

«What will we do now?» said the girls.

24

«There is no more light in the house and our labour is not finished yet. One of us shall run to Baba Yaga and borrow some light from her.»

«The pins in my lace give me enough light,» said the daughter who was weathing. «I don't have to go.»

«I don't have to go either,» said another daughter who was knitting stockings. «My needles give me enough light.»

«Then you shall go,» both sisters cried. «Go to Baba Yaga!»

And they pushed Vasilisa out of the room.

Vasilisa entered her small room and put the supper she had prepared before the doll, and said,

«Now my doll eat and listen to my trouble. I am sent for lights to Baba Yaga. Baba Yaga will swallow me!»

The doll ate the supper and it's eyes gleamed like two candles.

«Don't be afraid, Vasilisushka!» it said. «Go to where they sent you and always hold me with you. In my presence Baba Yaga will do no harm to you.»

Vasilisa got prepared, put the doll in her pocket, made the sign of cross and went to the thick forest. She walked and trembled.

Suddenly a rider galloped past her. He was white himself, dressed up in all white, and the horse's harness was also white. Daybreak came to the forest.

She went on ahead and a second rider galloped past her. He was red himself, dressed up in all red, and his horse was red. The sun rose.

Vasilisa was walking the whole night and the whole day. Only by the next evening she came up to the glade where Baba Yaga's hut stood.

The fence, surrounding the hut, was made of human bones, and the human skulls with eyes were on the spikes. There were human legs instead of gates and hands instead of bolts, and a mouth with sharp teeth in place of lock.

Vasilisa was frozen with terror and stood as if rooted to the ground.

Suddenly another rider passed by. He was black himself, dressed up in all black, and his horse was black. He galloped up to Baba Yaga's gates and got lost as if swallowed by the earth. Night came.

The eyes of all the skulls on the fence became to gleam and it was dark no more. The glade was bright as if it was day.

Trembling with fear she remained on the spot. She did not know where to run.

Soon a terrible thunder sounded from the woods. All trees were cracking, the dry leaves were crunching.

Baba Yaga showed up on the glade. She drove a mortar, hurried it on with a pestle and wiped her tracks with a huge broom.

She rode up to the gates, sniffed the air around her and yelled, «Fu, fu! It reeks with a Russian smell! Who is here?»

Vasilisa came up with fear to an old witch, bowed low and said, «It is me, grandmother! My stepsisters sent me to you for some light.»

«Very well,» said Baba Yaga. «I know them. But first live here a bit and work, then I'll give you the light. If not, I will eat you up right away!»

Then she turned to the gates and yelled, «Hey, my strong bolts, unlock! My wide gate, open up!»

The gate opened, and Baba Yaga entered the yard whistling. Vasilisa followed her and then everything closed up again.

Having entered the hut, Baba Yaga stretched herself out in her bed and told Vasilisa, «I am hungry. Pass over to me everything you find in the oven.»

Vasilisa lit a torch from those skulls on the fence and started bringing the food for Yaga from the stove. There had been prepared enough food for about ten people.

She brought some kvas, honey, beer and wine from the cellar. Everything was eaten and drunk by old witch. She just left some soup, a slice of bread and a piece of pork for Vasilisa.

Baba Yaga was about going to bed when she told Vasilisa, «Tomorrow, when I leave, see to it that you sweep the yard and the hut, cook the lunch, get the linen ready, then go to the granaries and sort the wheat out. If anything is not done I will eat you!»

Baba Yaga gave the orders and began to snore.

Vasilisa set the witch supper's leftovers before the doll, burst into bitter tears and said, «Eat, my little doll, and listen to my trouble. Baba Yaga gave a real job and threatens to eat me if I don't do it all. Help me out!»

The doll answered, «Don't be afraid, Vasilisa the Beautiful! Have your supper, pray and go to the bed. The morning is wiser than the evening!»

Vasilisa got up very early next morning, but Baba Yaga had risen already and was looking out of the window. The eyes of the skulls were going out. Then was a glimpse of the white rider and the day came.

Baba Yaga went out into the yard, whistled, and the mortar together with broom and pestle showed up before her. The red rider flashed by and the sun rose. Baba Yaga mounted the mortar and left the yard, hurrying it on by the pestle and wiping her tracks off by the broom.

When Vasilisa was left alone, she looked around Baba Yaga's hut and was amazed by plenty of everything. She stopped and thought what work to do first.

She looked around and saw that everything had been done. The doll was sorting out the last grains.

«Oh, my saviour!» said Vasilisa to her doll. «You have saved my life again!»

«All you have to do,» as the doll answered, getting into Vasilisa's pocket, «is to cook the dinner. Cook it with God's help and rest, for the sake of your health!»

By the evening Vasilisa served the table and waited for Baba Yaga. Dusk was lurking. The black rider glimpsed in the window and night came. Just the skull's eyes were gleaming.

The trees crackled, the leaves rustled. Baba Yaga was coming back. Vasilisa met her.

«Is everything done?» Yaga asked.

«If you please to see yourself, grandmother,» Vasilisa answered.

Baba Yaga examined everything, was upset a bit that there was nothing to get angry about, and said, «Very well, then!»

Then she cried out, «My true servants, my heart friends! Mill my wheat!»

Three pairs of hands appeared, took the wheat and dragged it out of sight.

Baba Yaga got stuffed and on her way to bed gave the orders to Vasilisa.

«Tomorrow you do the same work you have done today. But besides, take the poppy seeds from the granaries and take off all the ground specks from them. You see, somebody mixed it with ground out of malice.»

The old witch said this, turned to the wall and snored.

Vasilisa started feeding her doll. The doll ate and said the same like it had said yesterday, «Say you prayings to God and go to bed. The morning is wiser than the evening. Everything will be done, Vasilisushka!»

Next morning Baba Yaga mounted the mortar and left the yard again. Vasilisa and the doll did at once all the work.

The old witch returned home, examined everything and shouted, «My true servants, my heart friends! Squeeze the oil out of the poppy seeds!»

Three pairs of hands showed up, seized the poppy seeds and got out of sight. Baba Yaga sat down to dinner. Vasilisa stood behind while the witch was eating.

«Why aren't you talking to me?» said Baba Yaga. «Staying like a dumb.»

«I didn't make bold to talk,» answered Vasilisa, «but if you are not against, I would like to ask you about something.»

«Come on, ask! But not every question leads to a happy end. If you know much, you will grow old soon.»

«I want to ask you, grandmother, about what I have just seen. When I was coming to you, a rider on a white horse, dressed in all white overtook me. Who is he?»

«It is my bright day,» Baba Yaga answered.

«Then another rider overtook me. On a red horse and dressed in all red. Who is he?»

«It is my red sun!» answered Baba Yaga.

«But who is the black rider, who overtook me right at your gates, grandmother?»

«It is my dark night! All of them are my true servants.»

Vasilisa remembered about three pairs of hands and was keeping silence.

«Why aren't you asking more?» said Baba Yaga.

«This is enough to me. You, grandmother, told me yourself, that I would grow old soon if I would know much.»

«Good,» said Baba Yaga. «Why are you asking only about what you have seen beyond my yard, but never inside! I don't like my dirty linen to be out in public and as to the too inquisitive, I eat them! Now is my turn to ask you something. How do you manage to do the work I am giving to you?»

«My mother blessing helps me,» answered Vasilisa.

«Oh, I see now! Then get out of here, blessed daughter. I don't need blessed ones here.»

She dragged Vasilisa out of hut and pushed her out of the yard. Then she took one skull with burning eyes off the fence, put it on a stick and gave it to Vasilisa.

«Here is the light for your stepmother's daughters. Have it. That's what you are sent for.»

Vasilisa rushed away helped by the light of the skull, which died out only when the day broke out. By another night Vasilisa reached her house. Approaching the gates she was about to get rid of the skull.

«They perhaps need no light any more,» she thought.

But all of a sudden she heard a muffled voice from the skull.

«You shall not throw me. Bring me to your stepmother!»

She threw a look at her stepmother's house and without seeing any light in no one window decided to go there with a skull.

For the first time she was met with kindness. They told her that since she had left they had no fire at their house. They failed to strike a fire themselves and whatever light they were bringing from the neighbours was gone out just at the moment when it was brought into the house.

«Perhaps your fire will stay,» said the stepmother.

The skull was brought into the room. It's eyes were staring at the stepmother and her daughters and burning them. They would try to hide but wherever they would rush, the eyes found them everywhere. By next morning they were burnt to ashes. Only Vasilisa remained untouched.

In the morning Vasilisa buried the skull in the ground, locked up the door and went to the town. She asked some childless old woman to let her live in her house for a while. And she lived there, waiting for her father.

Some day she said to an old woman, «I am bored to sit workless, grandmother. Go and buy some flax, but let it be the best. I will spin at least.»

The old woman bought the best flax and Vasilisa got down to work. The work went on swimmingly, and the threads went out flat and thin as hair.

It is already much yarn. High time to start spinning, but there weren't any combs fitting Vasilisa's yarn and no one was able to make one. Then Vasilisa began to ask her doll.

The doll said, «Bring me some old comb, an old shuttle, and some horse's mane. I will contrive everything for you.»

Vasilisa got everything needed and went to bed. At night the doll made a nice wearing loom.

By the end of winter the linen was woven. It was so thin that could easily been pulled like a thread through a needle's eye. In the spring they bleached the linen.

Vasilisa said to an old woman, «Sell this linen, grandmother, and take the money for yourself.»

The old woman had a look at the linen and exclaimed, «No, my child. No one except the tsar shall wear such linen. I will bring it to the palace.»

The old woman went to the palace and paced up and down beneath the tsar's windows.

The tsar saw her and asked, «What do you need, old woman?»

«Your Majesty,» she answered. «I have brought remarkable wares to you. I don't want to show it to anybody except you.»

The tsar ordered to let her in. He was amazed when he saw the linen.

«What do you want in return?» asked the tsar.

«This is a gift to you, Tsar-father. It has no price.»

The tsar thanked her and let her go with many gifts.

The servants began to make shirts for the tsar out of this linen. The linen was cut out, but they couldn't find anywhere a seamstress who would have undertaken to sew it. They were searching for a long time.

Finally, the tsar called the old woman and told her, «You managed to spin and weave such a linen, so you must be able to sew shirts of it.»

«This was not me who spun it and wove, my Tsar,» she said. «This is work of my adopted child, who is a maiden.»

«So then let her sew it!»

The old woman returned to her house and told Vasilisa about everything.

«I knew always,» said Vasilisa, «that it would not pass by me.»

She locked up herself in her room and started working. She was sewing and never gave her hands to rest and soon a dozen shirts were made.

The old woman brought the shirts to the tsar's palace.

Vasilisa washed herself, combed her hair, dressed up and sat near the window. She was sitting and waiting for what would happen. She saw a tsar's servants coming to the old woman.

He entered the room and said,

«The tsar's will is to see the past master who made these shirts and to award her from his royal hands.»

Vasilisa went to the palace and appeared before the royal eyes. As soon as the tsar saw Vasilisa he fell in love with her forever.

«Never, my beauty,» said the tsar, «I shall part with you. You shall become my wife.»

He took Vasilisa by her white hands, sat her near him, and at once they married. Soon the merchant, Vasilisa's father, returned. He was happy to know her lucky fortune, and came to live with his daughter. Vasilisa took the old woman to live with her and always kept her doll and carried it in her pocket.

Tale of the Frog Tsarevna

Long-long ago, in ancient times there lived a tsar who had three sons. All of them grown up. Once the tsar told them,

«Children! Each of you make a bow and shoot. The woman who brings your arrow back will become your bride. The one who's arrow won't be brought back won't get married.»

The eldest son shot, and his arrow was brought back by a prince's daughter.

The middle son shot, and a general's daughter brought his arrow back to him.

But the smallest Tsarevich Ivan's arrow was brought back by a frog who held it in her teeth.

The eldest brothers were happy joyful but Tsarevich Ivan fell into thinking and wept.

«How will I live with a frog? To live a lifetime means more than to cross a field or to drag oneself over a river!»

He wept and wept but could do nothing and married a frog and all of them were wed in accordance with their local customs. The frog was sitting on a dish.

So they lived. Once the tsar ordered to bring him the gifts from the brides to see who of them was the most skillful. Tsarevich Ivan fell into thinking again and wept.

И. Билибинъ.

«What my frog is able to make! Everyone will be laughing.»

The frog just crept all around and croaked.

Then Tsarevich Ivan fell asleep. The frog went out in the street, threw off her skin, turned into a beautiful maiden and cried out, «Nannies and mammas! Make something!»

The nannies-mammas brought immediately a shirt of the finest workmanship. She folded the shirt and put it near Tsarevich Ivan and she herself turned back into the frog as if nothing had happened!

Tsarevich Ivan awoke, was very glad and brought the shirt to the tsar.

The tsar took the shirt, looked at it rapturously and said, «Well, this is really a shirt to be worn only on festive occasions!»

When the middle son brought the shirt, the tsar said, «This one is good to be worn in the hot bath!»

And from eldest son he took the shirt and said, «As to this one it's good only for the poor peasant hut.»

All the tsar's sons left and two of them were discussing and argueing,

«We shouldn't have laughed at Tsarevich Ivan's wife. She is not a frog, but some evil sorceress!»

The tsar than gave another order to his daughters-in-law that they should bake a bread each so that he could see who of them was the best in baking.

At first the oldest sons' wives made fun of the frog. Now they sent their nursemaids to spy on the frog and see how she would be cooking.

The frog got it, mixed up her dough, rolled it, hollowed out the stove and toppled the dough over right in the hale.

The nursemaids saw this, ran right to their mistresses, tsareviches wives, and those did it the same way.

But the cunning frog just fooled them. Right away she raked the dough out of the stove, cleaned everything and plastered up as it had always been the same.

Then she went out to the porch, threw the frog's skin off and cried out,

«Nannies and mammas! Bake immediately some bread the same as my father ate only on Sundays and holidays.»

The nannies brought the bread at once. She took it, put near Tsarevich Ivan and turned into a frog again.

Tsarevich Ivan awoke, took the bread and brought it to his father. Just then the tsar was examining what his older sons had submitted to him. Their wives had pushed the dough into the stove the way the frog had done it and what they received was fiddle-sticks.

First the tsar examined the eldest son's bread and sent it back to the kitchen. The middle son's bread was sent to the kitchen too.

Then it was Tsarevich Ivan's turn. He handed his bread to the tsar.

The father accepted it, examined and said, «This bread is indeed to be eaten on a holiday! Not the slab like my eldest daughters-in-law have cooked!»

After that it occured to the tsar to give a ball in order to see who of his daughters-in-law was the best dancer. All the guests and daughters-in-law got together, only Tsarevich Ivan's wife didn't come.

He fell into thinking, «Where can I go with a frog?»

And he burst into tears.

Then the frog said to him, «Don't cry, Tsarevich Ivan! Go to the ball. I'll be there in one hour.»

Tsarevich Ivan rejoiced a bit when he heard what the frog said and left. The frog threw off her skin and dressed up extraordinarily.

She went to the ball. Tsarevich Ivan was glad unspeakably and all the guests applauded to the beauty of his wife.

Everybody started eating and drinking. The tsarevna would bite a bone and put it in her sleeve. She would drink something and pour the rest into another sleeve.

The daughters-in-law saw what she did and did the same. They were putting bones in one sleeve, and the rest from the wine poured in another sleeve.

Then it was time for dancing. The tsar sent the elder daughters-in-law to dance, but they pointed to the frog. She at once took Tsarevich Ivan and went with him to dance. She would dance and dance, spin and spin, it was a real pleasure to look.

She waved her right hand and woods and waters showed up. She waved her left hand and various birds started flying all around. All were amazed. She quit dancing and everything disappeared.

The other daughters-in-law went also to dance. They wanted to repeat what the frog had done. Both waved their right hands and the bones flew straight into people, waved their left hands and the wine splashed into guests.

The tsar got angry.

«Stop it! Stop it!» he shouted.

The daughters-in-law quit dancing.

When the ball was coming to the end Tsarevich went home first, found somewhere there his wife's skin and threw it into the fire.

His wife came home and started looking for the skin, but didn't find it. It was burned.

She went to bed with Tsarevich Ivan and told him in the morning, «You had to wait very few and I would have become yours forever. But now God knows. Farewell! Look for me very far in the thrice ninth land, in the thrice ninth tsardom.»

And the tsarevna got lost.

A year passed and Tsarevich Ivan kept missing his wife. Next year he got prepared for the journey, solicited his parents for the blessing and was gone.

He had been walking for a long time when stumbled over a hut which stood with it's front side to the woods and with it's back to him.

He said, «Little hut! Little hut! Stand up the old way, the way your mother set you, with your back to the woods and with your front to me.»

The little hut turned around. He entered and saw an old woman sitting inside.

«Fu, fu! It was never heard of a Russian bone, never seen a glimpse of a Russian bone! Now Russian bone has come by it's own will. Where are you travelling, Tsarevich Ivan?»

«First, old woman, let me eat and drink. Then ask me about the news.»

The old woman gave him to eat and drink and led him to bed. Tsarevich Ivan told her, «Grandmother! I am coming to get Elena the Beautiful.»

«Oh, my poor child! So long haven't you been here. First years she was remembering you often. But now she doesn't remember you and I haven't seen her for a long time. Go now to my middle sister. She knows more than me.»

Next morning Tsarevich Ivan left and come to another hut.

«Little hut! Little hut! Stand up the way your mother set you, with your back to the woods and with your front to me.»

The hut turned around. He entered and saw an old woman sitting inside.

«Fu, fu! I was never heard of a Russian bone, never seen a glimpse of a Russian bone. Now Russian bone has come by it's own will. Where are you travelling, Tsarevich Ivan?»

«I am coming for Elena the Beautiful, grandmother.»

«Oh, Tsarevich Ivan, » said the old woman. «You are too late. She started forgetting you already and now she is about to marry someone else. She lives now with my elder sister. Go there, but look when you come close to the hut they will recognize you. Elena will be turned into a spindle and her dress will be pure gold. My sister will start winding the gold thread. When she finishes with her winding and put the thread in the box and locks it up, you must find the key, open the box, break the spindle, throw back the top of it and the bottom of it in front of you. And then Elena will appear before you.»

Tsarevich Ivan left. He found the third woman's hut and entered it. The old woman was winding the gold thread. She finished her work, put the spindle in the box, locked it and put the key somewhere.

He found the key, opened the box, took the spindle and broke it as it has had been said to him, threw the top back and the bottom in front of him. Suddenly Elena the Beautiful showed up before him and greeted him.

«How late you are, Tsarevich Ivan! I have almost married someone another.»

And another groom was about to show up. Elena the Beautiful took a flying carpet from the old woman, sat on it with and they were rushing like birds.

The other groom suddenly appeared and found that they had gone. He was also cunning!

He pursued them. He chased and chased and about only ten yards to get them failed. On the carpet they flew into Russia, but he some way was not allowed to Russia. He returned back.

41

They came home. Everybody was glad unspeakably and they began to live happily and they were prospering to the glory of all people.

Перышко Финиста Ясна-Сокола.

Tale of the feather of Finist, the bright Falcon

Once upon a time there lived an old man who had three daughters. The eldest and middle sisters were women of fashion, but the youngest one was taking care about the housekeeping.

One day the father decided to go to town and asked his daughters what present would like to get each of them.

The eldest daughter said, «Buy me some linen for a dress.»

The middle daughter asked about the same.

«And what would you like to receive, my beloved daughter?» he asked his youngest.

«Buy me a feather of Finist, the Bright Falcon, my dear father.»

The father said good-buy to his daughters and went to town.

He bought the linen for his elder daughters, but failed to find anywhere a feather of Finist the Bright Falcon.

He returned home and his elder daughters were happy to receive new garments.

«But I couldn't find a feather of Finist the Bright Falcon for you,» he said to his youngest.

«So, let it be,» she said. «May be next time you will be more lucky and find it.»

The elder daughters cut out their linen, sewed the new garments and laughed at their youngest sister. But she kept silence all the time.

Again the father decided go out to town and asked, «Well, my daughters, what kind of present would you like to receive?»

The elder daughters asked to buy kerchief for each and the youngest said,

«My dear father! Buy me a feather of Finist the Bright Falcon.»

The father went to town, bought two kerchiefs, but never saw a feather.

He returned home and said, «Oh, my dear daughter! This time I haven't found a feather again.»

«Never mind, father. May be next time you'll be more lucky.»

For the third time the father was about to go to town and asked his daughters what to buy for them.

The eldest sisters said, «Buy earrings for us».

But the youngest said again, «Buy me a feather of Finist the Bright Falcon.»

The father bought the golden earrings and began to look for the feather. Nobody heard anything about it. He became upset and left the town. As soon as he crossed the town's gate he met an old man who carried a small box.

«What are you carrying, old man?»

«A feather of Finist the Bright Falcon.»

«What do you want to get for it in exchange?»

«Give a thousand.»

The father paid the money and hurried home with the little box.

His daughters met him.

«My beloved daughter,» the father said to the youngest, «Finally, I have bought the present for you. Take it!»

The youngest daughter all but jumped with joy. She took the box and started kissing and fostering it. She pressed it tightly to her bust.

After supper everybody went to bed to their rooms. The youngest also came to her room and opened the box. The feather of Finist the Bright Falcon flew out at once, struck against the floor and a young tsarevich showed up before the maiden. And they began to talk to each other sweetly and tenderly.

The sisters heard them and asked, «Who are you talking to, little sister?»

«To myself,» she answered.

«Open up, then!»

The tsarevich struck himself against the floor and became a feather again. She took the feather, put it in the box and unlocked the door. The sisters entered, looked around and found nobody.

No sooner they had gone, the pretty maiden opened the window, drew out a feather and said, «Fly a bit, my feather, in the wide field. Have a work till the proper time comes.».

The feather turned into a bright falcon and flew away.

Next night Finist the Bright Falcon flew to his maiden. And they began to talk to each other cheerfully. The sisters heard them and run to their father at once.

«Father! Our sister has somebody and he visits her at night. Even now he is at her room and they are speaking with each other.»

The father got up and went to his daughter's room, but the tsarevich by this time had turned into a feather already and flew into the box.

«Ah, you mischievous girls!» the father scolded his elder daughters. «Why are you accusing her meanly? You'd better watch yourself!»

Next day the sisters decided to use cunning. In the evening, when it was dark outside, they put the ladder, gathered sharp knives and needles and stuck them on their sister's window frame.

At night Finist the Bright Falcon flew. He kept on beating against the window but failed to fly in. Just cut his wings.

«Farewell, my sweet maiden,» he said. «If you decide to look for me, then go beyond the thirtieth land and the thirtieth tsardom. First you will wear out three pairs of iron shoes, break three iron crooks and gnaw away three wafers made of stone. Then you will find me.»

But the maiden kept on sleeping. Although she heard these speeches in her sleep, she was unable to get up.

Next morning she woke up, looked around and noticed knives and needles stuck in the frame and blood draining from them. She waved her hands.

«Ah my Lord! My sisters must have killed my beloved friend!»

Right away she got ready and left her house.

She ran to a blacksmith's house, hammered three pairs of iron shoes and three iron crooks, provided herself with three wafers made of stone and hit the road in search of Finist the Bright Falcon.

She walked and walked, and wore one pair of shoes, broke one crook and gnawed away a stone wafer.

She came to a hut and knocked at the door,

«Host and hostess! Accomodate me for a night.»

An old woman answered, «You are welcome, lovely maiden! Where are you going, little dove?»

«Oh, grandmother. I am looking for Finist the Bright Falcon.»

«Oh, lovely maiden. This is a long way to walk!»

In the morning the old woman said, «Now go to my middle sister. She will give you good advice. And this is my present to you — a silver wheel for spinning and a golden spindle. When you spin a tow, you will draw out a golden thread.»

Then she took a clew, rolled it along the road and told the girl to follow it. She thanked the old woman and followed the clew.

Either a long or a short time it took, but the second pair of iron shoes was worn out, the second crook was broken and the wafer made of stone was gnawed away. Finally a clew led her to a hut.

She knocked at the door and said, «Kind hosts! Give a shelter to a lovely maiden from the dark night!»

«Welcome, come in,» an old woman answered. «Where are you going, lovely maiden?»

«I am looking for Finist the Bright Falcon, grandmother.»

«Long way you will have a to go.»

In the morning the old woman gave her a silver dish and a golden egg.

«Go now to my elder sister. She knows where to find Finist the Bright Falcon.»

The lovely maiden said farewell to the old woman and hit the road again. She walked and walked. The third pair of iron shoes was worn out, the third iron crook got broken and the third wafer made of stone gnawed away. The clew rolled up to a small hut.

The wanderer knocked at the door and said,

«Kind hosts! Shelter me from the dark night.»

Again an old woman went out.

«You are welcome, little dove! Come in! Where are you going and where does your road lead?»

«I am looking for Finist the Bright Falcon.»

«Oh, it's really a hassle to find him! He lives now in a certain town and he married the wafer maker's daughter there.»

In the morning the old woman told the maiden,

«This is a present for you — golden tambour and a needle. You just hold the tambour and the needle will be embroidering itself. Now go with God's help and let the wafer's maiden hire you as her maid.»

It was done as it was told. The lovely maiden came to the wafer maker's house and was hired as a maid. She was working much and quickly. Heating the stove, carrying water, and cooking meals. The wafer maker was happy watching her working.

«Thank God,» she told her daughter, «we hired a maid obliging and kind. Never needs to be told what to do!»

And the lovely maiden finished her work, took the silver spinning wheel and a golden spindle and began to weave. She was weaving and the thread, which was coming out, was of pure gold.

The wafer maker's daughter saw this and asked, «Ah, lovely maiden! Will you sell this toy of yours to me?»

«Perhaps I will.»

«What's the price?»

«Let me spend one night with your husband.»

The wafer maker agreed.

«No problem,» she thought. «I will give my husband a sleeping potion, but we will become rich with the help of this spindle.»

But Finist the Falcon wasn't home then. He was flying in blue skies all day and returned home by night.

They sat down to supper. The lovely maiden served the table looking at him all the time, but he never recognized her.

The wafer maker's daughter mixed the potion with his drink, sent him to bed and said to the maid, «Now go to his room and drive the flies off him.»

The lovely maiden was driving the flies off him and sobbing bitterly.

«Awake! Get up, Finist the Bright Falcon. I, the lovely maiden, have come to you. Three pairs of iron shoes I have worn out, three iron crooks I have broken, three stone wafers gnawed away while searching you!»

But Finist slept and felt nothing. The night was gone.

Next day the maiden took the silver dish and rolled the golden egg on it. Many golden eggs were rolled out. The wafer maker's daughter saw this.

«Sell this toy to me!» said the wafer maker's daughter.

«Good, buy it.»

«And what about the price?»

«Let me spend one more night with your husband.»

The wafer maker's daughter agreed again.

And Finist the Bright Falcon was again flying all day in the blue skies and returned home only by night.

They sat down for supper. The lovely maiden served the table and kept looking at him. But he looked as if he had never known her. Again the wafer maker's daughter gave him some potion with his drink and sent the maiden to drive flies off him.

And that time the lovely maiden was sobbing and driving the flies off him, but he heard nothing.

On the third day the lovely maiden took out the golden tambour and the needle was embroidering itself. And the traceries were so marvellous nobody had seen before. The wafer maker's daughter couldn't tear her eyes away.

«Lovely maiden! Sell this toy of yours to me!»

«I don't mind.»

«What's the price?»

«Let me spend the third night with your husband.»

The wafer maker's daughter agreed again.

By night Finist returned home. His wife poured the potion to his drink again, sent him to bed and ordered the maid to drive flies away from him.

The lovely maiden was driving flies away from him and kept saying, «Arise, Finist the Bright Falcon. I, the lovely maiden, have come to you. Three pairs of iron shoes I have worn out, three iron crooks I have broken, three wafers, made of stone, gnawed away while I've been looking for you, my beloved!»

But Finist the Bright Falcon kept on sleeping and felt nothing.

She was sobbing and trying to awake him for a long time. But suddenly a tear dropped on his cheek and he awoke instantly.

«Ah! Something burned me,» he said.

«Finist the Bright Falcon! I have come to you. I have broken three iron crooks, worn out three iron pairs shoes, gnawed away three wafers made of stone. This is the third night I have stood over you and you never wake up!»

Only then Finist the Bright Falcon recognized her and was so glad that could say nothing.

And they together left the wafer maker's house.

In the morning the wafer maker's daughter found that there was neither her husband nor the maid in the house. She started complaining to her mother and she ordered to get the horses ready and they rushed to pursue them.

They drove and drove, visited all the three old women, but didn't overtake Finist the Bright Falcon. Neither him nor his traces.

Finist and his beloved maiden reached her father's house. He struck himself against the damp earth and turned into a feather. The lovely maiden took him, hid in her bosom and went to her father.

«Ah, my beloved daughter! I thought already you weren't existing in this world. Where have you been that long?»

«I went to pray to God.»

And it happened right close to Holy Week. So the father and his elder daughters were about to go to matins.

«Well, my beloved daughter,» he said to his youngest, «get ready and let's go. It is such a fine day now.»

«Father! I have nothing to put on.»

«Put on our garments,» the elder sisters said to her.

«Ah, my sisters. Your dresses don't fit me. I'd better stay home.»

The father with the elder daughters went to the church. And the fair maiden took her feather out. It struck against the floor and turned into a nice tsarevich.

The tsarevich whistled from the window and the remarkable dresses and a carriage appeared.

They entered the church and stood before everybody and people marvelled at them, what a beautiful couple had come, real tsarevich and tsarevna.

When the matins were coming to an end they went out before everybody and went home. Carriage and dresses disappeared as if they had not existed. The tsarevich turned into a feather.

The father and the daughters returned home.

«Oh, sister! You haven't come with us but we saw a handsome couple in the church, tsarevich and tsarevna.»

«Very well, sisters. You told me, so it is as if I had been there myself.»

Next day the same thing happened again. When the tsarevich and tsarevna left the church and sat down in the carriage, the father of the lovely maiden went out of the church and saw by his own eyes the carriage pull up to his house.

The father returned home and started questioning his youngest daughter. She said, «I have to tell you the truth. There is no choice.»

She took out the feather. The feather struck against the floor and turned into the tsarevich. Then they married and the feast was rich!

I have been to this wedding. The wine trickled down my mustache but didn't get into my mouth.

Maria Morevna

Many years ago there lived Tsarevich Ivan in a certain tsardom. He had three sisters: Tsarevna Maria, Tsarevna Olga and the third, Tsarevna Anna. Their parents had died.

When they were dying, they instructed their son, «The first bride of your sister must become her husband. Do not keep them for a long time with you.»

The Tsarevich buried his parents and went to the garden for a walk together with his sisters. All of a sudden a black cloud covered the sky, terrible storm broke out.

«Let's go home, sisters!» said Tsarevich Ivan.

As soon as they entered the palace a thunderstorm broke out. The ceiling was split in two parts and a bright falcon flew into the room. He struck himself against the floor, turned into a brave tsarevich and said, «Hail, Tsarevich Ivan! Before I was coming here as a guest, but now I've come as a suitor. I want to marry your sister, Tsarevna Maria.»

«If she loves you, I'm not going to keep her. Let her go with God's grace.»

Tsarevna Maria agreed and the falcon took her to his tsardom.

Days followed days, hours followed hours. A whole year passed as if it had not existed.

Tsarevich Ivan took two sisters and went for a walk into a green garden. A huge black cloud crossed the sky again and a thunderstorm broke out.

«Let's go home, sisters,» said the Tsarevich Ivan.

As soon as they came to the palace, the ceiling was split in two parts and an eagle flew into the room. He struck himself against the floor and turned into a brave tsarevich.

«Hail, Tsarevich Ivan! Before I had been visiting you as a guest. Now I came as a suitor.»

And he asked Tsarevich Ivan to let his sister Olga become his wife.

Ivan answered, «If she loves you, I am not against this marriage. Let her become your wife.»

Tsarevna Olga agreed and he married her. The eagle took her and brought to his tsardom.

Another year passed.

Once Tsarevich Ivan told his youngest sister, «Let's go out for a walk into a green garden.»

They walked for a while. Again the black cloud with a whirlwind arose and lightning flashed.

«Let's return home, sister.»

They returned home and no sooner they had sat down, a thunder rolled. The ceiling was split in two parts and the black raven flew in. He struck himself against the floor and turned into a brave tsarevich. The first and the second tsareviches were nice, but that one was even nicer.

«Well, Tsarevich Ivan. Before I had been coming to see you as a guest, but now I came as a suitor. Let me marry Tsarevna Anna.»

«I do not forbid. If she loves you, let her become your wife.»

Tsarevich Ivan remained alone. A whole year he lived without his sisters, and he became bored.

«I will go and look for my sisters,» he decided.

He got ready for the journey and hit the road. He walked and walked and saw a host of soldiers lying all dead in the field.

Tsarevich Ivan asked, «If anybody is alive, let him respond me! Who ruined this great army?»

An alive man answered him, «All this great army was killed by Maria Morevna, the beautiful queen.»

Ivan Tsarevich went ahead and came to white tents in the wide field. Maria Morevna, the beautiful queen, went out and met him.

«Hey, Tsarevich Ivan! Where God is taking you? You are travelling by your will or against it?»

Tsarevich Ivan answered her, «Brave tsareviches never travel against their will!»

«Well, if you do not hurry, have a rest at my tents.»

Tsarevich Ivan accepted the invitation gladly. He spent two nights at the tents. He fell in love with Maria Morevna and married her.

Maria Morevna, the beautiful queen, took Tsarevich Ivan to her tsardom. They lived together for a while and then the queen decided to start war. She left all the household in Tsarevich Ivan's charge and ordered him, «Go everywhere, keep an eye on everything, but never look into this lumber-room.»

But Tsarevich Ivan couldn't restrain. As soon as the queen left, he rushed immediately to the lumber-room, opened the door and glanced inside. And there Koshchey the Deathless was hanging chained with twelve chains.

He begged of Tsarevich Ivan, «Have a pity over me. Let me drink. Ten years I have been suffering here neither ate or drank. My throat is totally overdried.»

Tsarevich gave him a whole bucket of water. He drank it and asked for more.

«One bucket is not enough to quench my thirst. Give me more!»

Tsarevich Ivan gave him another bucket of water. Koshchey drank it and asked for a third one. After he had drunk three buckets of water he regained his former strength. He shook the chains and broke all twelve at once.

«Thank you, Tsarevich Ivan!» said Koshchey the Deathless. «From now you will never see Maria Morevna like you will never see your ears!»

And as a terrible whirlwind he flew out of the room. He overtook Maria Morevna, the beautiful queen, seized her and brought her away.

Tsarevich Ivan wept for a while, got ready for a journey and hit the road.

«Whatever may happen, I must find Maria Morevna!»

He walked one day, another, and at the third day's dawn he saw a marvellous palace. There was an oak near it, and a bright falcon sat on it.

The falcon swooped down, struck himself against the earth and turned into a brave tsarevich and cried, «Hail, my dear brother-in-law! Is God on your side?»

Tsarevna Maria ran out. She met her brother with joy, and began to ask him about his health and told him about her own life.

Tsarevich Ivan stayed three days with them and said,

«I can't stay with you for a long while. I have to search for my wife, Maria Morevna, the beautiful queen.»

«It will be difficult to find her,» the falcon said. «Leave your silver spoon here just in case. We'll be looking at it and remembering you.»

Tsarevich Ivan left his spoon with the falcon and hit the road. He walked and walked. At the sixth day's dawn he saw a palace which was even nicer than the first one. There stood an oak near the palace and on the oak sat an eagle.

The eagle flew down from the oak, struck himself against the ground, turned into a brave tsarevich and shouted, «Arise, Tsarevna Olga! Our beloved brother is coming!»

Tsarevna Olga ran to them immediately. She began to kiss and embrace her brother, asked him about his health and told him about her life.

Tsarevich Ivan spent three nights with them and said, «I can not stay with you any more. I am looking for my wife, Maria Morevna, the beautiful queen.»

The eagle told him, «It will be too hard to find her. Leave your silver fork here. We will be looking at it and remembering you.»

He left his silver fork and went on. He walked one day, another. When the third day broke out he saw a palace even more remarkable than the first two. There was an oak near the palace, and a raven sat on it.

The raven flew down, struck himself against the floor and turned into a brave tsarevich and cried, «Tsarevna Anna! Come out quickly. Our brother is coming!»

Tsarevna Anna ran out, met her brother with joy. She began to kiss and embrace him, asked him about his health and told him about her life.

Tsarevich Ivan spent three nights with them and said,

«Farewell! I must go to look for my wife, Maria Morevna, the beautiful queen.»

The raven said to him, «It will be hard to find her. Leave your silver snuff-box with us. We will be looking at it and remembering you.»

Tsarevich Ivan gave his silver snuff-box to them, said farewell and left. On the third day he reached Maria Morevna.

She saw her beloved, rushed to him, then burst into tears and said,

«Ah, Tsarevich Ivan! Why did you unlock the lumber-room and let Koshchey the Deathless out?»

«Forgive me, Maria Morevna! Do not recall the past. Let's instead go with me while Koshchey the Deathless is away. Perhaps he won't overtake us.»

They got ready and left.

Koshchey hunted at that time. On his way home at night his horse stumbled under him.

«What's wrong with you, hungry jade? Do you feel a trouble?»

The horse answered, «Tsarevich Ivan came here and took off with Maria Morevna.»

«Can we overtake them?»

«We should sow wheat, wait till it grows, reap it and thresh, grind it into flour, bake five breads and set out after eating all it. Even then we will overtake Tsarevich Ivan and Maria Morevna!»

Koshchey started off and caught up with Tsarevich Ivan.

«Well, I will forgive you for the first time. You were kind to me and let me drink water. The second time I will forgive you too. But next time you won't be forgiven.

He took Maria Morevna from the Tsarevich Ivan and took her off. Tsarevich Ivan sat down on a stone and burst into bitter tears.

He wept and wept and returned for Maria Morevna. Koshchey the Deathless was away again.

«Let's go Maria Morevna!» he said.

«Ah, Tsarevich Ivan, he will overtake us again!»

«Let him catch us. At least we will spend one hour together.»

They got ready and took off. As soon as Koshchey returned, his horse stumbled under him again.

«Why are you stumbling, hungry jade? Do you feel something is wrong?»

«Tsarevich Ivan came here and he stole Maria Morevna.»

«Can we get them?»

«We must sow some barley, wait untill it grows, brew beer, get slushed, have a good sleep and after all go and catch them!»

Koshchey rushed to pursue them and caught up with them.

«Haven't I told you that you'll never see Maria Morevna like you'll never see your own ears!»

He took her off and brought back to his palace. Tsarevich Ivan remained alone. He wept and wept and returned to get Maria Morevna again. Koshchey was out then.

«Let us go quickly, Maria Morevna!»

«Ah, Tsarevich Ivan! He will reach us and chop you into pieces.»

«Let him chop me! I shall not live without you.»

They got ready and took off. As Koshchey the Deathless was coming closer to his house, his good horse stumbled under him.

«Why did you stumble? Do you fell any trouble?»

«Tsarevich Ivan was here and took Maria Morevna with him.»

Koshchey rode off, overtook Tsarevich Ivan and chopped him into little pieces and put them into a tarred cask. He strengthened it with iron hoops and threw it away into the blue ocean and carried off Maria Morevna.

At exactly that moment Tsarevich Ivan's silver, which he had left at the palace of his brothers-in-law, blackened.

«Ah,» they said, «some trouble must have happened to our brother!»

The eagle rushed to the blue ocean, caught the cask and dragged it ashore. The falcon flew for the water of life and the raven for the water of death.

All birds got together at the same place, broke the cask, took out the chopped pieces of Tsarevich, washed them and stuck to each other. The raven sprinkled them by the dead water, and the pieces grew to each other and rejoined.

The falcon sprinkled him with the water of life, Tsarevich Ivan got up and said, «Oh, how long I slept!»

«You would have slept even longer if it hadn't been for us,» his brothers-in-law answered. «Let's go visit us now.»

«No, my brothers. I must go and look for Maria Morevna.»

He came to her and asked, «Find out from Koshchey the Deathless where he had fetched so good and speedy horse.»

So, at the right moment Maria Morevna started asking Koshchey.

Koshchey told her, «Very far from here, at the thirtieth tsardom, beyond a flame river Baba Yaga lives. She has such a steed on which she flies the world over every day. She has many other such steeds. Three days I have served as her herdsman and no one steed was escaped. So as a reward one colt was presented to me.»

«So how did you manage to cross the flame river over?»

«I have such a kerchief that when I wave it to the right side three times, the highest bridge stands up and the flames can't reach it!»

Maria Morevna listened to what he said and repeated everything to Tsarevich Ivan. She managed to steal the kerchief from Koshchey and gave it to her beloved.

Tsarevich Ivan crossed the flame river and went to where Baba Yaga lived. He was walking for a long time without eating or drinking. He happened to meet some strange bird from foreign land with her young.

Tsarevich Ivan said, «I will eat one of your kids.»

«Don't eat him, Tsarevich Ivan,» the bird begged. «Some day I will become useful to you.»

He kept on walking and stumbled upon a beehive in the forest.

«Oh, I will eat some honey,» he said.

The queen bee answered him, «Do not take my honey, Tsarevich Ivan. Some day I shall be very useful to you.»

Tsarevich Ivan didn't take any and went on. Soon he met a lioness with a little whelp.

«I will eat this little lion's whelp at least. So hungry I am!»

«Tsarevich Ivan, do not take him,» the lioness begged. «Some day I shall be useful to you.»

«All right, let it be so!»

And he kept on plodding, still hungry. He walked and walked until he reached the hut of Baba Yaga. Eleven stakes with eleven human heads on each surrounded the hut.

«Hello, grandmother!»

«Hail, Tsarevich Ivan. Did you come by your own free will or some need brought you here?»

«I came to deserve a mighty steed, grandmother.»

«Try, tsarevich! You shall not serve a year here, but only three days. If no one of my mares escapes from you, you'll get one. If you fail to keep them, don't hold it against me, but your head will hang on the last stake.»

Tsarevich Ivan agreed. Baba Yaga fed him and let him drink and ordered to get down to work.

As soon as Tsarevich Ivan pulled the mares to the field, they raised their tails and scattered in all directions. Tsarevich didn't even raise his eyes, when they got out of

sight. He wept, grieved, set on the stone and fell asleep. It was day already when the foreign bird flew to him and woke him.

«Get up, Tsarevich Ivan! The mares are back now.»

The tsarevich got up and returned home. Baba Yaga was yelling that time at her mares. «Why did you return?»

«How could we stay in the meadow? Birds from all over the world swarmed up and almost pecked out our eyes.»

«All right, tomorrow instead of running in the fields, you'd better scatter in thick woods.»

The tsarevich slept that night, and in the morning Baba Yaga told him,

«Look, tsarevich! If only one of them escapes your rash head will be on the stake!»

He pushed the mares out in the field. At once they raised their tails and rushed to thick woods. Again tsarevich sat on a stone, wept and fell asleep. The sun set behind the forest. The lioness run to him.

«Get up, tsarevich! The mares have been gathered already.»

Tsarevich Ivan got up and went home. When he returned, Baba Yaga was shouting at the mares even more severely.

«Why have you returned home?»

«But what could we do? Wild beasts from all over world gathered together and almost tore us to small pieces.»

«Tomorrow you run into the blue ocean.»

Tsarevich Ivan slept that night. In the morning he was sent to herd mares again.

«If you loose even one of them, your rush head shall be on the stake.»

He drove the mares into the fields. At once they raised their tails and vanished from sight. They stood in the water up to their necks. The tsarevich set on the stone, cried bitterly and fell asleep. A bee flew to him when the sun set behind the forest.

«Get up, tsarevich! All the mares returned home already. But when you are back home, never show up before Baba Yaga. Go to the stables, hide behind the manger. There you will find a scabby colt lying on a dung heap. Steal him at midnight and escape from the house.»

Tsarevich Ivan got up, led his way to stables and hid behind the manger. Baba Yaga scolded and shouted, «Why have you returned again?»

«We couldn't help coming back. An innumerable number of bees flew together from all over world and began to stung us till blood!»

Baba Yaga fell asleep. Right in the middle of the night Tsarevich Ivan stole a scabby colt, saddled him and galloped to the flame river of fire. When he came to the shore, he waved his handkerchief thrice. All of a sudden, as if from nowhere, a high bridge hung over the river.

Tsarevich Ivan crossed the river and waved his handkerchief to the left side only twice. Very thin bridge over the river remained.

Next morning Baba Yaga arose. The scabby colt was nowhere in sight. She rushed to pursue them. She flew on her iron mortar as fast as she could, prodded it with an iron pestle and swept her traces away with a broom.

She flew up to the flame river, glanced at the birdge and thought, «Good bridge it is!»

She rode onto the bridge, but as soon as she reached the middle, the bridge broke down. Baba Yaga fell into the flame river and really had a cruel death!

Tsarevich Ivan fed his colt in the green meadows. It became a splendid steed.

The tsarevich came to Maria Morevna. She ran out, rushed to him and embraced him.

«How did Lord bring you back to life?»

«This way and that,» he said. «Come on! Let's go with me!»

«I am afraid, Tsarevich Ivan! If Koshchey overtakes us, you will be chopped into little pieces again.»

«No, this time he won't catch us! I now have a splendid steed which is as fast as a bird.»

They mounted the steed and galloped off.

As Koshchey was coming closer to his palace, his steed stumbled under him.

«Why are you stumbling, hungry jade? Are you scenting Ivan smell again?»

«He was here and carried off Maria Morevna.»

«Can we overtake them?»

«God knows! Tsarevich Ivan has now a mighty steed which is better than me.»

«No! Anyway I'll get them both!» said Koshchey the Deathless.

After a long time or a short time, he caught up with Tsarevich Ivan, jumped off his horse's back and tried to hack him with his sharp saber. At that moment Tsarevich Ivan's steed kicked Koshchey the Deathless with it's hoof and smashed up his head. The tsarevich finished him with his iron mace.

After that he set a pile of woods, made a fire, burned Koshchey and let his ashes to the wind.

Maria Morevna sat on Koshchey's horse and Tsarevich Ivan on his one. First they visited the raven, then the eagle and, finally, the falcon. Wherever they came, they were met joyfully.

«Ah, Tsarevich Ivan! We didn't even hope to see you again. But you didn't waste time, indeed. Such a beauty as Maria Morevna has no peer in the world.

They stayed there for some time, had a great feast and rode off to their own tsardom. Having arrived, they lived long and prospered.

Tale of the White Duck

Once a certain knight married a beautiful princess. He hadn't managed to enjoy, to talk and to listen to her sweet speeches enough, when he had to leave for a long journey. He left his wife on the strangers' hands.

What could they do? It's said that one can't leave forever in embraces.

The princess wept much, many words were told her by the knight. He ordered her to never leave the high chambers, not to deal with evil people and not to listen to their evil speeches. The princess promised him to obey and he was gone. She locked up herself in her chamber and wouldn't leave.

After a long or a short time, a woman came to see her. So simple and kind she seemed to be!

«Why are you getting bored? Go out to have a look at God's world. At least walk in the garden, dissolve your grief, clear up you head.»

The princess was refusing for a long time, but finally she thought, «This is no trouble in walking in the garden!» And she went to take a walk.

The crystalline water was sprinkling in the garden.

«The day is so bright and hot,» the woman said. «The sun is shining, and the water is cool. Won't we bathe here?»

«No, no! I don't want it.» But then she thought, «There is no trouble in having a bath.»

She took off her frock and jumped in the water. As soon as she plunged in the woman hit her on the back.

«You swim now as a white duck,» she said.

And the princess turned into a white duck.

The witch at once put on her frock, painted herself and sat down to wait for the knight.

No longer than the puppy had barked and the bell had rung, she rushed to meet the knight. Kissed him and fondled. The knight was overjoyed, stretched his hands towards her and didn't feel the change.

At that time the white duck laid eggs and hatched the ducklings. Two of them were healthy and the third one was a weakling. And they grew into good children later.

She raised them and they began to swim in the river, catch little fish, sew little robes, jump onto the banks and glance at the meadow.

«Oh, don't go up there, kids,» she told them.

But they didn't listen to her. One day they would play on the grass, an other day they would romp in the meadow, and every day they went farther till they reached the prince's courtyard.

The witch felt their scent and recognized them, grinded her teeth. She let them drink and eat and sent to beds. Then she ordered to sharpen the knives, to hit the boilers, to set the fire.

Two brothers felt asleep, but the weakling was ordered them by their mother to be carried in their chests because he could catch a cold. And he didn't fall asleep and heard everything.

At night the witch came to their door and asked, «Are you sleeping, little children, or not?»

The weakling answered, «We are sleeping and not sleeping. We think that somebody wants to slaughter us. They are putting hazel logs into fire, heating the boilers, sharpening the steel knives.»

«They are not sleeping!»

The witch left, walked a bit and returned to their door.

«Are you sleeping, little children, or not?»

The weakling answered again, «We are sleeping and not sleeping. We think that somebody wants to slaughter us. They are putting hazel logs in the fire, heating the boilers, sharpening the steel knives.»

«Why it is the same voice all the time?» the witch thought and opened the door. Both brothers were sleeping. She touched them with her dead hand and they died.

Next morning the white duck called her children, but heard no response. She felt pain in her heart, she waved her wings and flew to the knight's courtyard.

In the courtyard both brothers were lying. Both cold as dead bodies, white as kerchiefs.

The white duck rushed to them, spread her wings over them, howled with the mother's voice:

> Quack, quack, my little kids,
> Quack, quack, my little doves!
> I raised you in need,
> I fed you with tears,
> I never slept at dark nights,
> I didn't eat a sweet lump.

«Do you hear, my wife, oddly things are going on! The duck is speaking with a human's voice».

«You seem to hear this! Let the duck out of the courtyard!»

The duck was driven out but she flew back to her kids again.

> Quack, quack, my little kids,
> Quack, quack, my little doves!
> We were undone by an old witch,
> By an old witch, by a hurtless bitch,
> That mean shake-in-the-grass
> She took away your father,
> She put us in the swift stream,
> Who is my husband and your father,
> She drowned us in a running river,
> And she turned us into white ducks.

«What could this mean?» the knight thought. «Catch this white duck for me.»

Everybody rushed to catch the white duck. But the duck was flying and didn't let anybody touch her.

The knight ran out himself and she fell into his hands.

He touched her wing and said, «White birch tree stay behind me and the lovely maiden stay in front of me.»

The white birch stood in behind him and a lovely maiden showed up in front of him. And he recognised his young princess at once.

A magpie was caught at once and it was ordered to fill two phials, which had been tied up to it, with water of life and water of speech.

The magpie flew there and brought the waters. The kids were sprinkled by the water of life and they shaked their wings. They were sprinkled by the water of speech and they began to speak.

So the knight obtained his family again. They began to live good and prosper and forget the bad times.

As to the witch, it was tied up to the horse's tail and dragged over a wide field. Where her leg was torn off, a fire iron grew out. Where the hand was torn off, a rake grew out. Where her head was torn off, bushes grew.

Many birds swooped down and pecked the witch's flesh off. The wind dispersed the bones. Neither trace or memory of her remained in the world!

Russian fairy tales

Complited by A. Afanasiev
Illustrations by I. Bilibin
Translated from Russian by A. Zamchuk

ООО Издательство «Литература»
115407 Москва, ул. Судостроительная, д. 40
Лицензия ЛР № 064527 от 11.04.96 г.

Подписано в печать 10.02.2000 г. Формат 60x90 1/8
Гарнитура Гельветика. Бумага офсетная № 1.
Печать офсетная. Объем 9 п. л. Тираж 5000 экз. С-032. Заказ № 3572.

Тверской ордена Трудового Красного Знамени полиграфкомбинат детской литературы им. 50-летия СССР Министерства Российской Федерации по делам печати, телерадиовещания и средств массовых коммуникаций.
170040, г. Тверь, проспект 50-летия Октября, 46.